You Can
Change
Your
World!

You Can Change Your World!

Creative Ways to Volunteer and Make a Difference

Sondra Clark

Fleming H. Revell
A Division of Baker Book House Co
Grand Rapids, Michigan 49516

Published by Fleming H. Revell
a division of Baker Book House Company
P.O. Box 6287, Grand Rapids, MI 49516-6287
www.bakerbooks.com

Printed in the United States of America

Library of Congress Cataloging-in-Publication Data is on file at the Library of Congress, Washington, D.C.

ISBN 0-8007-5852-8

Contents

Introduction

Have you ever wanted to make the world a better place, but didn't know how? I have. In fact, about a year ago, feeling that way led me to quite an adventure.

I'm a typical middle school kid who likes to play soccer, ski, and be with my friends. I live in an ordinary neighborhood like most of you probably do. Then I went to Africa. Yes, Africa.

After the twenty-hour airplane trip, we landed in Uganda. I was there as a spokeschild for Childcare International. Childcare International is a Christian relief organization that asks people in the United States to sponsor a child in Africa or another region with developing countries. When families sponsor a child, that child's life changes forever. Instead of sleeping on the dirt floor, they have a bed. Instead of living by themselves in a cow-dung hut, they sleep in a dry building. Instead of eating one small meal a day, they get adequate food. Instead of only wishing they could go to school, they get both uniforms and an education.

When I visited Kenya and Uganda, I was shocked at the poverty. Children my age came up to me, begging for money. I felt spoiled because my spending money  was more than their parents made in several months. The roads were dusty and had huge potholes. We got jostled around as the driver swerved so he wouldn't hit the biggest holes. I remember stopping at a gas station. At least, I think it was a gas station—it had only one pump. Our driver, John, went inside a ramshackle building to get help. Now this wasn't your typical self-serve gas station. The attendant came out with a metal bar. He unlocked the pump and used the bar to hand crank the gasoline into the car. Then he locked the pump so no one could steal any gas!

The poverty we saw in Africa was overwhelming, yet the people overwhelmed us with their kindness. In one remote village, they presented us with three one-gallon jars of honey. This represented hours of hard work—they were giving us their valuable food! One lady gave my mom an intricate beaded necklace. She made my dad a beaded watchband. Since beads are very hard to come by where she lived, this meant she sacrificed her valuable beads to make us gifts.

Every place we visited, the people sang and danced for us. We could tell they had practiced many hours. One of the songs they sang went like this:

> We are very happy to see you here today,
> We are very happy to see you at this location,
> We are happy, oh so very happy.

A group of girls performed a dance for our family. They took tiny steps and had quick hip motions. Then it happened! They asked me to join them! Somehow my dancing looked like a bad version of the Macarena. All 150 kids who were watching burst out laughing as I danced.

An emotional part of my trip was meeting Annette, the twelve-year-old girl I sponsor. Both her parents are dead, and she lived with her grandmother for a while. Soon, her grandma couldn't take care of Annette. After I sponsored her, she got to move to one of the group homes run by Childcare International. Even though we are about the same age, our lives couldn't be more different:

Her entire wardrobe was two dresses.
She'd never seen hot water coming from a faucet.

She went to a school with dirt floors and no windows. She had never watched television.

Yet in spite of these differences, Annette and I became friends. We got to cut a special cake and serve it. It was only a small nine-inch cake, so every child got a small piece about the size of a marshmallow. One of Childcare's staff members had baked the cake at her home on the mainland. She brought it on a five-hour boat ride to Bugala Island. Since there is no electricity on the island, baking anything is very difficult. The children hardly ever get sweets, so even a small bit of cake was a treat. I also brought some new

clothes for Annette. We wore matching shirts and hats. It was fun sitting together for meals. I know Annette's life is better because we sponsor her.

After seeing all the children who don't have sponsors, I decided to do what I could to help. When I got back home, I began speaking at churches, showing slides of my trip to Africa. Then I asked people to spend $30 a month to sponsor a child. It's exciting to have people come up after my presentation and look at pictures of kids who are available to be sponsored. I especially like it when I see people a few months later and hear them say, "I got the sweetest letter from my sponsored child. It made me cry."

You might say, "How can I make a difference in the world? I'm just an ordinary middle school kid with a messy locker." That may be true, but God can use your specific talents and skills. Peggy Clark, a vice president at DePaul University, said, "I have only recently discovered the best gift of all—that I can make a difference by making my life a gift to others." Your smile, your acts of kindness, and your life can improve the world.

This book is about how you can help make this world a better place. You may not be able to go to Africa, but you can make a difference in your own unique way. We'll look at ways to volunteer, share, and help others. You can improve the world by improving your home, school, and community. So let's get going!

Part 1

It All Starts at Home

Can you imagine this as a typical conversation at your house?

Sondra: "Good morning, Mom. I'm almost ready for school. I made my bed, brushed my hair, and I'm wearing the pink-and-yellow polka-dot sweater Grandma knit me."

Mom: "That's nice. I made you your favorite strawberry waffles with fresh strawberries. Do you need me to finish your homework for you?"

Sondra: "Thanks, but I got all my homework done yesterday. I also did an extra credit report for English."

Mom: "You're the best daughter in the world!"

Sondra: "And you're the best mom in the world!"

Dad: "We must be the happiest family in the world!"

Sondra: "Oh, I better go catch the bus. I don't want to be late for another day that's full of learning."

Dad: "Don't take the bus . . . I've hired a limousine to take you to school."

Sondra: "Thanks, Dad, I'll use the phone from the limo to call and tell you how much I love you."

If your family talks like that, you certainly are one of a kind! Most families aren't that sickeningly sweet to each other. Families love each other, but they also argue, spill juice on the carpet, and miss the school bus. God gave each one of us a very special family. (Though at times you wonder why God put you in the same family as your annoying little brother!) No matter what size or type of family you have, you also have the power to be a helpful, positive family member.

Remember the Titanic? You've probably heard or read about this British luxury liner sailing on its first voyage. The experts said the Titanic was "unsinkable." The builders must have been very confident in the Titanic's safety, because only twenty lifeboats were stored on deck. On April 15, 1912, the Titanic

Quiz Time

Making a difference . . . that's a wide-open statement. It means many things. Put a check mark by the statements that show a *positive* way to make a difference in your home.

_____ Trip your brother as he walks by your chair.

_____ Make your mom a cup of tea as she pays bills.

_____ Send a thank-you note to your dentist after he takes off your braces and you have a great smile.

_____ Forget to give your dad an important phone message.

_____ Offer to help at your little sister's soccer practice.

_____ When your mom asks you to walk the dog, give it a token effort by going to the end of the driveway and back again.

_____ Delete your dad's spreadsheet on the computer without asking if you should save it.

_____ Thank your parents for driving you to ballet class.

Hopefully it's obvious you can change the world by making a positive difference right at home!

hit a huge iceberg and began sinking in the Atlantic Ocean. About two thousand people were on board . . . with only twenty lifeboats. People jumped into the first available lifeboats and pushed out into the water, away from the huge sinking ship. Some lifeboats had extra room, but the passengers didn't take time to load more people. Soon all twenty lifeboats drifted in the cold water. The passengers in them could hear people in the water, crying for help. But the passengers knew the lifeboats were in danger of tipping over if they went back to rescue more people. So they got farther and farther away from the Titanic.

The passengers in Lifeboat #14 made a dangerous decision. They saw that they had extra room and decided to go back. They followed the sounds of people calling for help. According to witnesses, "A precious few were saved." Those in Lifeboat #14 did what they could to help. My pastor, Steve Mason, tells this story several times a year. He points out the importance of doing what we can to help people, whenever we can.

As you read about my trip to Africa, some of you were ready to pack your bags to go over and meet my African friends. Others of you probably thought, "That's not for me!" We all know God gives us special talents. We can use our talents in many different ways. Not everyone gets to visit Africa or be in a lifeboat rescuing drowning people. But you *can* help people wherever you are.

One way to make the world a better place is to start at home. Have you heard the phrase, "Charity begins at home"? That means you can accomplish just as much "good" at home as in an exotic location. Sometimes it sounds more glamorous to help needy children in Africa than to help your little sister with homework. But God doesn't need you to leave home to help others. Making a positive impact at home is just as important as making a positive impact in Timbuktu.

Mother Teresa helped "the poorest of the poor" in Calcutta, India. She would get letters from people asking if they could help her by coming to work with the dying people she cared for. She would reply that they should stay home and help people in their own homes and communities. She frequently said, "Calcutta can be found all over the world if you have eyes to see." She stressed the fact that people don't have to come to India to make a positive change in the world.

Treat Your Family Like Company

Home is a place to relax, where we can wear mismatched pajamas, sing at the top of our lungs, and burp when we feel like it. But sometimes we get too relaxed in how we treat our family members. When guests come over, do you treat them the same way you treat your brother or sister? Probably not. Most likely you act politely and offer to hang up their coats. But when they leave, it's back to mismatched pajamas.

Accept a personal challenge and try to treat your family as if they were company. Yes, they'll be shocked, but try it and see what happens. Say please and thank you. Compliment your mom's cooking. Try to ignore your little brother's annoying habits. Make an effort to do something nice for your family.

Did You Know?

The Journal of Early Adolescence (a magazine most kids never read) told about a study of 133 families. They found that kids who have close relationships with their parents are more "emotionally healthy." That means they feel better about themselves and can cope with problems better. So go ahead . . . have fun and enjoy being with your parents!

Try This!

- Make a centerpiece for the dinner table.
- Do your chores without being asked.
- Help your sister with her school project.
- Let your dad choose what he wants to watch on TV without complaining.
- Plan a family activity to do together.
- Write a note to someone in your family, telling them you love them.
- Ask your parents if there is anything you could do to make their day better.
- Ask your parents if you could have a family meeting to discuss ways to have more fun together as a family.

Sondra's Ways of Making a Difference

1. My mom and I have a notebook that we use to write to each other. One night she'll write some-

thing to me and leave the notebook on my pillow. The next day I write her a note and put it on her bed. This is a way to encourage each other and reflect on the day. Sometimes it's easier to write things down than to say them face-to-face.

2. Our kitchen pantry was a mess of cans and boxes of food. It was hard to find my favorite lentil soup. (Yes, I love lentil soup. I even eat it for breakfast.) To make it more organized and to help my mom, I took everything out of the cupboards. Then I organized everything into canned vegetables, fruits, soups, tomato sauce, etc. I even made a chart of where everything should go. Now it's easier to find what we need.

Put Yourself in Your Family's Shoes

So often we hear about people doing great and fantastic things, such as discovering a cure for a rare disease. That's wonderful, yet ordinary kids like you can do things that still make a positive impact on your family. Practice making a difference in your home, and soon you'll be ready to make a difference in the world by finding a cure for the common cold.

You may watch reruns of *The Brady Bunch* and say, "Our family could never be as perfect as the Bradys." You're right. The Bradys had professional writers telling them what to say and set designers who always kept the house looking immaculate. (Their pantry was never a mess.) None of it was real. When I was a preschooler, I did a toy commercial for Mattel. The scene was supposed to be a sunny day in a park. In reality, we were in a warehouse with plastic grass, fake flowers, and a recording of birds in the background. Families in real life do get into arguments and have clothes lying on the floor. (At least my family does!) Just remember, you are a real family, not a made-up family like the Bradys. Do your part to make your family a better place to be. Hey! Maybe someday there will be a TV show based on your family!

You may have heard the phrase, "Don't judge someone unless you've walked a mile in their shoes." This goes for family members also. Try to look at people in your family and think about why they act the way they do. When your dad comes home tired from work, try to understand why he says, "I'm too tired to play basketball now. Let's do it after dinner." Put yourself in his shoes and realize he just drove through a heavy traffic jam coming home.

This strategy is called empathy. You try to understand how another person is feeling. When you were a toddler and got fussy and cranky, your mom understood you were tired. She empathized with your feelings, read you a book, and put you down for a nap.

The next time your sister fights with you, take a minute and think about why she's acting so mean. Maybe she's getting a cold or she got a bad grade on her spelling test. Once you realize why she's acting the way she is, you're more likely to be kind to her.

These ideas aren't glamorous. Yes, it would be more exciting to be trekking through the Amazon jungle, trying to find the one plant that will cure cancer. And that would be a wonderful accomplishment. Yet in

God's eyes, it's also a great accomplishment to help your little brother practice being a goalie so he can make the soccer team.

Later on in this book, I'll give you resources and ideas to help improve the world in more "glamorous" ways. But for now, let's stick with practical ways for you to make the world a better place by getting along with your family.

Have you ever been to camp? You probably had crazy counselors who planned all sorts of wild activities. They organized games, helped you put on skits, and told funny stories. Here's your chance to be a Junior Counselor and plan some fun things for your family to do together. Put on your camp T-shirt, grab a whistle, and get your family involved in these camp activities.

Try This!

1. Organize a nature scavenger hunt. Give every family member a list of things to find as you walk through the park. Include things such as the smallest acorn, a heart-shaped rock, a twig that forms a letter, etc. Collect items in a plastic bag. See who can find the most items.
2. As you eat dinner, make a rule that you can only sing. No talking allowed. It's hard to stay mad at your brother if you have to sing to him, "Michael, pass the mashed potatoes."

3. Make a family video and send it to a distant relative. Film each other giving a tour of the house or pretending to be interviewed on a TV show.
4. Plan a mini-marshmallow roast. Light a candle and poke toothpicks into miniature marshmallows. Slowly roast them over the candle flame. Smash the melted marshmallow between two small pieces of graham crackers and a few mini-chocolate chips. Yummy!
5. Plan a Christmas in July night (or Valentine's Day in October). Get out decorations, make cards, and celebrate a holiday at an unusual time of year.
6. Speaking of holidays, why not celebrate some of these crazy holidays?

January 30:	National Popcorn Day
April 6:	National Twinkie Day
June 19:	Garfield the Cat's birthday
July 13:	International Puzzle Day
August 9:	Smokey the Bear's birthday
November 18:	Mickey Mouse's birthday

Grandparents

Each year, the Sunday after Labor Day is Grandparent's Day. See what you can do to make your grandparents feel special. I bet your grandparents would love to tell you what life was like when they were kids. Get a tape recorder and record what your grandparents have to say. If they live close by, plan a picnic together. Call them if they live far away. When I was little, I would draw a picture and fax it to my grandma. She would add something to the picture like a bird or a pretty flower and fax it back to me. Then I'd add something. We kept faxing the picture back and forth until it was full of all sorts of interesting things. Many stores carry Grandparent's Day cards, but I bet you could be creative and make your own. Grandmas and grandpas love getting homemade cards. You could even nominate your grandparents for "Grandparent of the Year" on *www.grand parents-day.com*.

When you are with your grandparents, ask questions. What was their school like? Did they have lots of toys? What chores did they do? You'll form a closer relationship with your grandparents by listening to their experiences. My grandma and great-grandma lived in Germany during World War I and World War II. Here's a report I wrote after interviewing my great-grandma.

My "OMA"

She never used a computer. She never spoke on a cell phone or used an ATM machine. Yet she did live through two world wars and experienced the Holocaust. She nursed her husband out of the face of death. She even taught herself to drive at the age of sixty-five.

My great-grandmother, Marie Viktora, was born at home on November 17, 1905, in the little town of Gorlitz, Germany, located near the Polish border. Marie's father worked for the local opera house, building elaborate scenery. Marie liked to visit her father at work and see the things he built. During those days, people walked everywhere, but they still enjoyed coming to see shows. A few people used streetcars to get around.

Each morning when Marie woke up, her mother had fresh rolls for breakfast. Then Marie would walk to school. All the boys were in one group of classes and the girls in another. They had to go to school on Saturday and only had six weeks of summer vacation.

At noon, instead of going to the cafeteria for lunch, Marie walked back home. Families ate their main meal at noon. While Marie worked in school in the morning, her mother had been busy doing the daily shopping. They didn't have large stores like Costco, so people went to small specialty stores. Marie's mother would first go to the baker for fresh bread. Then she'd walk next door to the butcher for meat. Marie's favorite meal was liver dumpling soup, so her mother would buy fresh liver. Vegetable stalls stood on every street corner. Even on cold days, Marie's mother would walk or ride her bike to the stores to get the daily supplies. When she arrived home, she needed to cook the meal. Apartments had no electricity. A coal stove gave heat and was used for cooking.

In 1914 Marie's life changed when World War I began. It was not a happy time for the family. During the days, Marie walked to the edge of town to pick old potatoes left in the ground from the farmer's harvest. Her hands were constantly dirty, and she'd get tired from carrying potatoes. The potatoes soon ran out, and Marie's family was forced to eat dandelion leaves. Her mother carefully picked nettles to make nettle soup. A little bit of flour and some wild onions gave the soup some flavor. Soon there wasn't even nettles or grass to eat.

In 1918 the war ended. Marie's father was killed on the last day of the war. After WWI more changes happened. Germany was divided into two parts. One half was ruled by Russia and the other half by America. Communists now ruled the people in Chemnitz. Many people tried to escape from communism.

The years went by. And unfortunately WWII began. Marie married Hans, and they had three girls: Helga (my grandma), Hanne, and Irene. They ran a small vegetable and fruit cart. Marie took her little girls to her work every day. Life was hard, but people survived.

Hans had to go serve in the army. He even had to bring his own truck. He fought in France and then had to fight in Russia. The Russians captured Hans and put him in a prisoner of war camp. Every day he had to chop down big trees and load them onto a boxcar. He didn't even have gloves. All the prisoners had to work long hours with very little food and in unbearable conditions. After several long years, he was released and came home. Marie didn't recognize him. He was given a can of potato peelings as food on the trip home. He saved all the peelings to give to his three daughters at home.

The war ended, and Hans slowly regained his strength. Marie fed him thin soup to build up his strength. They soon began a new business when Hans found an old truck in a dump. He fixed it up and started a delivery service. The business grew to include several trucks. Marie did all the bookkeeping. When Hans died in 1964, Marie moved to the United States to be with her daughter Helga, my grandmother.

Marie was very active. When she was eighty years old, she complained that the people at the Senior Center were too old and slow to go on walks with her. She loved to walk and would walk miles every day. Employees at stores in downtown Bellingham knew her and would wave as she walked by. If she didn't like their window display, she'd stop and tell them how to improve it. Everyone knew her as Oma.

At times Oma had a hard life, but she always looked for ways to make the best of the situation. She died on January 2, 2000. The ninety-four years of her life were filled with many changes. She saw Germany taken over by Communists and then brought back to a democracy. She saw slot machines run by computers, and she used cars instead of horses for transportation. Most of all, I got to spend the first eight years of my life knowing this remarkable, smart, and caring woman.

Since we're talking about how to make the world a better place, think how your grandparents would feel if you wrote a story about them. Type it up, draw a nice picture, and present your grandparents with their very own book. They'll treasure it forever.

Family Fun

Do you get the *Weekly Reader* at school? They did a survey and asked 1,500 kids, "What makes a happy family?" Can you guess their answers? The main answer from kids was, "Doing things together."

What kind of things does your family like to do together? If you want to make a difference at home, try helping your parents plan a special activity. Families get busy; we all know that. Spending time with grandparents or even your own mom and dad takes effort. But every family can find ways to enjoy being together.

My family loves musical theater. We're lucky enough to go to New York every year when my mom speaks at a conference. Then we see three Broadway musicals in four days! We've also figured out a way to get the actors' autographs. After each show, we find the stage door (usually in an alley) where the actors go in and out. We wait there for the actors to go home. I usually wear a sweatshirt from the show and hold a black permanent marker. When the actors come out the door, I turn around and ask them to sign the back of my sweatshirt with the marker. I have a great collection of autographed shirts.

At home, we play a game called "Broadway Baby." My parents will give me the name of a famous musical like *Gypsy, Lion King,* or *Annie.* I go upstairs and dig through all my costumes to come up with something that makes me look like the character in the play. Then I perform songs from that play for my parents. Naturally, they clap and cheer and give me another musical to do. (I think they like the quiet time as I'm working on putting my costumes together.) Your family may not be into musicals. That's okay. The important thing is to find things to do together.

I bet your family likes candy. Here's a fun game to play. Can you use these clues to help you name each candy? (Answers are on page 119.)

1. A trio of buddies
2. Superman's real name
3. Large, good-looking man
4. Small hills
5. I can't remember the name
6. Charlie Brown's admirer
7. Happy nut
8. Bumpy street
9. Ex-NY Yankee
10. Red Planet
11. The day a worker likes best
12. Young coin maker
13. Bovine flops
14. Point total in a game

Craft Projects

Our family has fun doing crafts together. Just remember, crafts don't have to be all cutesy wootsy with frilly ribbons. There's a great book by Dan Reeder called *Make Something Ugly for a Change.* He gives ideas for papier-mâché projects that show three-headed creatures and snakes that are curled around a birthday cake. Mix up a batch of papier-mâché and create your own family "Ugly Item."

Recipe for papier-mâché (so you can make something really ugly!)

Recipe #1: Mix equal parts of liquid starch and water. Stir well. Dip strips of torn newspaper in solution. Squeeze excess moisture out. Wrap saturated newspaper strips around your papier-mâché object. Let dry and repeat with several layers.

Recipe #2: Mix together one box wallpaper paste according to directions on package. Now add a teaspoon or so of water to get the consistency of runny pudding. Dip newspaper strips just like in directions above.

How about making an amusement park for birds? Get wood and empty plastic bowls or cups. Have everyone design feeding stations or unique perches for the birds. Set your creations out in the yard and see how the birds like them.

If it's snowing, your birds and small animals would like a Nature's Delight Restaurant. Make a regular snowperson and "decorate" it with food. String popcorn and cranberries as a giant necklace. Sprinkle birdseed on the snowperson's hat. Give your snowperson a polka-dot shirt by sticking raisins all over the body. Use apple slices to make a smile and pinecones dipped in peanut butter and birdseed for the eyes. Don't forget a carrot nose! Birds and squirrels will enjoy your outdoor restaurant.

Here's an easy, off-the-wall craft. Do you like to play Ping-Pong? Give everyone permanent colored markers and have them decorate the Ping-Pong balls so they look like bloodshot eyeballs. It adds interest to a normal game!

If you want some more traditional craft projects, try these ideas:

Decorate some frames: If you are like my family, you take lots of pictures. Instead of keeping the pictures in a photo album, decorate some frames and proudly display all your smiling faces. Begin with a plain cardboard or wooden frame. You can find inexpensive frames at dollar stores. Just make sure the frame is smooth. Here are three ways to decorate them.

1. If you have a great picture of your dog, create a dog-bone frame. Simply glue the tiny-sized dog biscuits onto the frame. Let glue dry. Then use a paintbrush to cover them with a coat of

Mod-Podge, which preserves the biscuits and makes them shiny.

2. Have some puzzles with missing pieces? Instead of throwing out the puzzle, use the pieces for a great frame. Spread the puzzle pieces on newspaper outside. Use spray paint and paint all the pieces. If you don't have spray paint, just use whatever paint you have to paint each puzzle piece. Let dry. Using permanent markers or small paintbrushes, draw designs on each painted puzzle piece. You can make polka-dot flowers, ladybugs, etc. Spread glue on the back of each puzzle piece and glue to the frame. Go ahead and overlap the pieces. You'll have a distinctive, one-of-a-kind frame.

3. Have a picture of you swimming or fishing? Make a fish frame. Glue tiny goldfish crackers around the edge of the frame. Cover with Mod-Podge again. Let dry and add the picture of you with the trout you caught at camp last summer.

This isn't really a craft, but it is fun to play with. Make a batch of Sondra's Slimy Goop. Follow these directions to create a stretchy, slimy, gooey substance.

- Mix 1/2 cup very cold water and 1/2 cup Elmer's glue.
- Stir well.
- In a separate bowl, mix 1/2 tablespoon Borax with 1/4 cup very hot water. (Not boiling water.

Also, Borax is a cleaning agent found in grocery stores by the laundry detergent.)

- *Add a few drops food coloring to water/Borax mixture (optional).*
- *Slowly add hot water mixture to glue/water mixture.*
- *Stir. Suddenly goop forms!*

For best results, knead with your hand until mixture is smooth and pliable. You'll love stretching and playing with the goop. Try to keep it off the carpet and furniture, though. This keeps for weeks in a covered container in the refrigerator.

Ask a parent to check if your local newspaper gives away free end rolls of newsprint. You'll end up with a huge roll of paper. Put the paper on the floor. Take turns tracing around each person's body. Cut out your paper body and then use crayons or markers to add hair, clothes, and other details. When the bodies are finished, switch paper bodies. Write something positive about that person on their "shirt." Keep switching papers until all family members have written on all the shirts. Proudly display your thin bodies!

This Could Be You ...

Do you have a barn? If so, your family could volunteer with this Christmas activity. Linda and Dave Sieloff of Stockbridge, Wisconsin, use their barn to re-create the birth of Jesus. Their church is too small to hold all the people for Christmas Eve service. The Sieloffs let people come to their barn. While the choir sings and the pastor tells about Jesus' birth, people sit on hay as barn animals move around. Everyone gets a real feel for the first Christmas.

Action Plans

Plan #1

Plan a "Week of Making a Difference." Ask other family members to participate and choose from the ideas below (or come up with your own ideas). All these suggestions are easy and inexpensive. Try them and see what happens!

Monday: Decorate your little brother's or sister's lunch bag. Slip an "I love you" note in your dad's pocket.

Tuesday: Ask if you can make a special dessert for dinner. Offer to do an extra chore around the house.

Wednesday: Since your parents drive you places, vacuum the car. See if a brother or sister needs help with homework.

Thursday: Don't hog the remote control today! Make a special centerpiece for the dinner table.

Friday: If you share a room with a brother or sister, clean up their side of the room. Give your parents a spontaneous hug.

Saturday: Make a card for a family member and leave it on their pillow. Do a secret good deed for someone in the family.

Sunday: Plan a family activity to do together. Have family devotions in the evening—reading by candlelight.

Plan #2

Welcome new neighbors. If you see a moving truck pull into your neighborhood, go over as a family and welcome the new people. Give them directions to the best pizza parlor in town. Invite them to church or a walk through the neighborhood.

Plan #3

Order a catalog from S&S Worldwide. Just have an adult call 800-243-9232 or order online at *www.ssww .com*. They have great craft kits that include all the supplies you need for making sand monsters, kaleidoscopes, and crazy critter frames, and they even have decorate-your-own-kite kits. They also have an assortment of Christian craft kits.

Plan #4

Organize a "Family Mailbox Party" night. Collect all sorts of art supplies such as markers, ribbons, glue, yarn, paper scraps, and buttons. Give each person in your family a manila envelope. Ask them to put their name on it and decorate it in a clever way. (My dad decorated his envelope and wrote, "I want LOTS of notes in here!!!") When everyone has finished their colorful masterpieces, use thumbtacks and put them outside everyone's bedroom door. It's fun to write short notes and stick them in each other's paper mailboxes. Maybe you'll write a note to your sister saying, "I'm sorry I yelled at you last night." Perhaps you'll put a note in your mom's mailbox saying, "Thanks for making my school lunch every day." It's an easy way to help your family get along better.

Plan #5

Be a Super Spy! Have you ever wanted to be a secret agent? I have! Here's your opportunity. You don't even need a costume. Pick a day when you act as a spy. Your mission is to find ways to help out at home . . . without being asked. When your dad comes home from work, offer to hang up his coat. Is your mom looking for her glasses? Try to find them. Your mission is to see a need and take care of it. A good spy isn't obvious. Just keep an observant eye out to find ways to make your home a better place to be.

See, making your home a better place isn't all that hard. Hopefully your whole family will try some of these ideas. You might all find yourselves as happy as the Brady Bunch!

Volunteer Together

Families that do things together can be an inspiration to others. If your neighbors see you helping mow an elderly neighbor's yard, they'll be more likely to help out also. Talk with your family about what you can do to make your neighborhood a better place to live. Are you good on the computer? Find a free web-hosting company and put together a neighborhood web site. Keep it updated with news about Mrs. Johnson's lost dog or the upcoming garage sale at the Carlson's house. Put together a decorated box or bag with maps of the area to give to a family that moves into the neighborhood. Plan a special event like a street party or a neighborhood block party. People feel safer knowing their neighbors. Your family can be a role-model family for others. Jesus said, "Let your light shine." By helping neighbors know each other better, your family can light the way to building a close-knit community.

My dad really believes in "being a light." He has our entire house outlined in white lights. A huge lighted American Flag hangs above our garage door, and during the 2002 Olympics, he built the Olympic rings out of colored lights. He turns the lights on every night, and the house "blazes" with lights throughout the neighborhood. My mom turns them off when he's not looking!

Speaking of lights . . . our small-group Bible study planned to drive a van to Warm Beach Christian Conference Center to see their Lights of Christmas Festival. The festival has incredible lights, plays, storytellers, and craft booths. It is about an hour from our house. The night of the event, several families called saying they couldn't make it. We decided to cancel the trip. Our family thought about two little girls who belonged to our group. We knew they would be disappointed and too young to understand about the cancelled trip. We came up with an alternate plan. A short distance from our house was a small train that traveled through a field decorated with colored lights. It wasn't as fancy as the Lights of Christmas, but it was perfect for Ashayla and Amanda. We picked them up and had a fun time squeezing into a tiny train and riding by lighted displays of Snow White and the Seven Dwarfs and Humpty Dumpty's house. It was a nice feeling to see how our family could make these two girls happy.

As you look at ways to make a positive difference in your family, look at ways you can volunteer together. There are many easy ways that your whole family can get involved in helping others. One family noticed a new apartment complex being built for low-income families. The apartments were nice but had few flowers or bushes. The family got permission to plant seeds, shrubs, and flowers. Often, the families living in the apartments came out to help. Everyone worked together, adding color to the landscaping.

Each year, the National Arbor Day Foundation encourages people to plant trees. For $10, you can get ten trees sent to your house that are designed to grow in your climate. Just send a check to National Arbor Day Foundation, 100 Arbor Ave., Nebraska City, NE 68410. Plant the trees in your yard or ask the Parks department if your family can plant the trees in a local park.

Your family might want to get involved with National Family Volunteer Day. This is one day when families are encouraged to do something special and volunteer for at least one day. You can get more information from the Points of Light Foundation at *www.pointsoflight .org*. I filled out the form, telling about my fund-raising efforts for Childcare International. They selected me as a winner! On February 15, 2002, my picture and story were posted on their web site. I also got a letter from President Bush, congratulating me on my volunteer work. Have you done something to make your community a better place? Don't be shy. Nominate yourself or your family and see what happens.

Did You Know?

The Vanier Institute of the Family studied families that volunteered together. Here are some of the benefits they discovered:

Volunteering gives families the chance to be together.

Volunteering develops family pride.

Volunteer work gives families a sense of purpose or belonging.

Volunteer work can show families new ways of problem solving.

Some families make huge sacrifices in order to volunteer. Can you imagine giving up a trip to Disneyland to fix up a run-down house? Families signing up with Christmas in April (202-483-9583) go to poverty-stricken areas and help repair homes and improve the community. One family helped rebuild a woman's house. It had rotten floors, a leaking roof, and broken windows. For a week, they did hard work to help give someone else a nice place to live.

Other families volunteer by "digging." The Passport in Time program is run by the U.S. Forest Service (800-281-9176). Families learn to be junior archaeologists and help with excavation sites around the United States. They dig for artifacts and record what they find.

Try This!

Okay, you know the benefits of volunteering, but just exactly what can you do? Some families are too busy to volunteer on a regular basis. If you have really young brothers or sisters, it might be hard to serve food at a homeless shelter. Here's a variety of ideas. Look them over together and see which ideas will work for your family.

- If you go on vacation or your parents travel, collect the hotel soaps and shampoos. Donate them to a women's shelter.
- If you are at a restaurant and the staff give you a package of crayons, don't open them. Save them to give to kids that might not have as many crayons and markers as you do.
- Collect old newspapers and give them to animal shelters to line animal cages.
- Have a garage sale and donate a portion of the money to charity.
- Collect all the loose change in your house. Roll it up in paper rolls (or use one of the coin counters available at many grocery stores). Give a portion of the money to charity.
- Offer to do cleanup at your church. You could pick up litter, plant flowers, or clean the toys in the nursery.

- Donate videos you've outgrown to a children's hospital or to foster homes.
- Offer to take an elderly neighbor's dog for a walk.
- Collect unused eyeglasses. You can take them to LensCrafters, who will then clean them and give them to the needy.
- Do you have membership to local science museums or children's museums? Donate your guest passes to foster families or women's shelters.
- Collect all your pretty Christmas cards. Send them to St. Jude's Ranch, a home for abused children. The kids make spending money by recycling the cards. St. Jude's Ranch, 100 St. Jude's St., Boulder City, NV 89005.
- Assemble some Bedtime Snack Sacks. Decorate paper lunch bags and fill them with a juice pack, granola bar, raisins, and other nonperishable food. Deliver the sacks to a food bank so kids can have a snack before they go to bed.
- Is your pet well trained? Call a local nursing home and see if the residents would like to see your family pet.
- Invite someone who lives alone to come over for dinner after church.
- Offer to help preschool Sunday school teachers prepare lessons by cutting out flannel board pictures or preparing craft projects.

- Special Olympic teams always need volunteers. See if you can help with practices and meets or tournaments.
- Ask your family to buy a live Christmas tree. That way you can plant it after Christmas.
- Is someone in your family good at fixing things? Ask friends to donate old bikes. Work together repairing and cleaning the bikes to give to needy children.
- This one means a sacrifice: Some families decide to give each other fewer presents during the holidays and use the extra money to provide presents to a family facing hard times.

These are some ways you could volunteer as a family. On a day-to-day basis, there are plenty of ways to help make your home a better place to be. Here are more ideas to work on together.

- Save electricity by turning off lights you don't need.
- Try to conserve water. Take shorter showers and turn off the water while brushing your teeth.
- Set up recycling bins for paper, plastic, aluminum cans, etc.
- Get a book at the library on how to build a compost heap. Make a family project out of composting.

- When you go shopping, look for items that don't have extra packaging.
- Keep a litterbag in the car . . . and use it!
- Reduce pollution by using your car as little as possible. Yes, it means you have to walk or car-pool, but it helps keep the air fresh.
- If you have weeds along the sidewalks, pull them out instead of using toxic sprays.
- Set up a backyard wildlife sanctuary. You can get details and a complete low-cost idea kit from: Backyard Wildlife Sanctuary, 16018 Mill Creek Blvd., Mill Creek, WA 98012. If you want to get started helping wildlife before you get the kit, you can do a few things now. Birds need water, so keep fresh water available. Set out various types of birdhouses to attract different birds. Get your neighbors interested in backyard habitats. If several backyards provide natural vegetation, water, and a source of food, more birds and butterflies will soon appear.

Action Plan

Have your family volunteer for the Fresh Air Fund. You probably live in a house or apartment with a dishwasher, computer, and hot water for a shower. It's easy for you to ride your bike or play in a nearby playground. There are many kids right in the United States who live in the inner city. It may be dangerous for them to go outside. Broken bottles may be lying by the playground equipment. The families may not have enough food. The Fresh Air Fund matches up disadvantaged children in New York with families like yours. During the summer, New York kids get to spend a few weeks living with host families. The kids from New York are shocked to be able to go outside and not worry about gangs or other scary things. Fresh Air children are between six and eighteen years old. You get to show them all the fun things you do, like going to museums and having picnics at the lake. You can get more information about the program from *www.freshair.org*. Having a Fresh Air child live with you shows them a new environment and gives them a chance to be a regular kid.

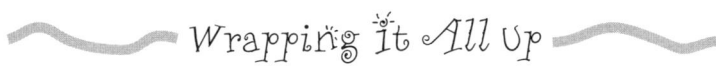 Wrapping It All Up

Making your home a better place:

H Help even if you are not asked. Look for ways to help other family members. Don't forget to help family pets. Your dog would probably appreciate a nice long walk.

O Organize family activities. Plan a picnic or read to each other. Don't always wait for your parents to suggest ideas.

M Make an effort to be kind. Instead of thinking about yourself, see how you can be kind to others. Remember the people in Lifeboat #14? They made a huge effort to rescue drowning people.

E Enjoy your family. Sure, your dad tells corny jokes and your older brother teases you. But show support and enthusiasm for what other family members do. Even if your sister plays Pee-Wee softball, act as if she's in the World Series!

Part 2

Making Your School a Better Place

Have you ever read the *Little House on the Prairie* books? Laura and Mary went to school in a one-room schoolhouse without electricity or an indoor toilet. All the kids up to eighth grade were in one room. In fact, the whole school only had about fifteen students. Even with a small school, Laura and Mary had ways they could make a positive difference. They helped bring in wood for the stove. When bratty Nellie picked on other kids, Laura helped defend the underdog.

Your school probably has more than fifteen students in one class, let alone the whole school. This gives you plenty of opportunities to be a positive influence. If Laura could help someone in her tiny school, you can certainly help at your school.

Think about it. You go to school for six hours a day for at least thirteen years. That gives you lots of time to make your school a better place. Some people think it is up to the principal and teachers to make the school great. You are a major part of what happens at your school. One of the best ways to improve your school is to be a positive role model!

If you are homeschooled, you can still make a difference! Probably the biggest way to help someone is to cooperate when your mom or dad gives you an assignment! Homeschoolers have an advantage over kids in traditional schools, because they can volunteer during the day. Try getting a few of your homeschooled friends together to play bingo at a senior center or lead songs at a preschool. One group of middle school homeschoolers took care of kids at a women's shelter in the mornings while the moms were in a counseling session. You could even put together a flyer describing volunteer opportunities for other homeschoolers. You can be a role model for other kids even if you go to school at home.

Tiger Woods, in his book *Start Something*, said, "Being a role model means more than having others look up to you. A role model is someone who accepts responsibility for getting others to do great things." You know you are a very special person with wonderful talents. Help other kids see that they have tal-

Did You Know?

In my state of Washington, you can still visit a one-room schoolhouse. The Waller Road School in Puyallup used to have fourteen students from first through eighth grade. The toilet, called an outhouse, was outside. If you needed to use it, you had to hold up one or two fingers to show just exactly what you needed to do in the outhouse! The teacher during that time earned $60 a month.

ents and skills also. Best of all, get those people to use their talents in positive ways.

It's easy to cut down your school and its activities. Have you heard kids say, "That art contest is so stupid!" or "Who wants to be in a school play?" or "Why can't we have better food in the cafeteria?" Instead of going along with negative comments, show others how to look on the positive side.

Let's pretend that next Friday is Western Dress-Up Day at your school. You hear kids saying, "Western Day? How lame! I'm not dressing up." Which of these things could you do to get other kids involved?

1. Don't dress up. You might be the only one and then people will laugh at you.
2. Wear overalls to school. Tie a bandana around your neck to add to the Western look.
3. Invite some friends over the day before and put costumes together. Everyone can bring any

extra straw hats or gingham blouses for kids who don't have costumes.

If you circled number 3, you are definitely a role model for others. Answering 2 was also good. Often kids want to dress up, but they think they'll be the only ones. If you get a bunch of kids to participate, it's more fun for everyone. When you take the lead, other kids will follow. This makes the school a better place as more and more kids get involved.

Show you are a role model by turning in your homework on time. Use Post-it notes to remind you about upcoming tests or special projects. If the school has a homework hotline, use it! Learn a few memory tricks. Do you know the difference between principle and principal? A principal wants to be your "pal." Get it? I'll always remember all nine planets because a teacher taught us a mnemonic (memory) trick. The first letter of each word stands for a planet. All you have to do is remember, "My very educated mother just served us nine pizzas."

My/Mercury
Very/Venus
Educated/Earth
Mother/Mars
Just/Jupiter
Served/Saturn
Us/Uranus

Nine/Neptune
Pizzas/Pluto

Hopefully you'll have a test on the planets next week at school. Then you'll be able to use this mnemonic trick!

Most kids in the United States have so many opportunities at school they never take advantage of. I was lucky enough to visit schools in Kenya and Uganda. I noticed their academic standards were higher than ours. Second graders were doing fractions at a fifth-grade level. I was shocked that most kids spoke three languages: English, Swahili, and their tribal language. What is more amazing is that they learned these languages without computers, worksheets, or language specialists. When I first walked into a classroom, it seemed so bare. They had concrete walls without posters or brightly colored artwork. Students didn't have desks like ours. They sat on wooden benches with a narrow board on top to write on. I could go on and on about what the schools don't have. They *don't* have:

Computers
Electricity
Playground equipment
Expensive sets of encyclopedias

But they *do* have:

A positive attitude

Caring, dedicated teachers (who teach from 8:00 A.M. to 5:00 P.M.)

Inquisitive minds

The ability to sing, dance, and learn

Teachers couldn't just go to the educational school store and buy supplies. They carefully cut out letters from worn-out rubber flip-flops. They made their own books from small pieces of paper. One teacher used paper and a box to try to explain what a TV was.

The people were incredibly friendly. At every place I went, they greeted us with welcome songs and dances. At one of the schools, children walked five miles, many of them barefoot, just to see us. On the Ssese Islands, they wanted to decorate the children's school for us, but they didn't have any crepe paper or streamers. Instead, they unwound toilet paper and strung that from the buildings. I brought along pencils that said "Jesus Loves You." They were so excited to get one small gift.

Now that I'm back home, I have a greater appreciation for what I have. My school, like yours, has books, computers, and indoor plumbing! If children in Africa are happy with a pencil, then I should do all I can to have a positive attitude at my school.

Quiz Time

Do you feel like school is boring? Do you end up going home and watching cartoons after school? Here's a test to see if you need to get more involved in school activities.

_____ Do you spend most of your time alone?

_____ Do you watch more than two hours of TV after school?

_____ Do you eat junk food while watching TV?

_____ Are you relieved when the bell signals the end of the day?

_____ Do you often complain about being bored?

If you answered yes to most of the questions, it probably means you aren't very involved at school. This doesn't mean you have to be a super-enthusiastic rah-rah cheerleader, but it might be an indication that you should look into joining one club or activity to help give you a feeling of being connected to your school.

Action Plan

Call a local 4-H office and see how you can get involved. Most kids think 4-H clubs are only for kids living on farms. Not anymore! 4-H programs cover everything from computers to raising guide dogs for the blind. 4-H clubs place a strong emphasis on volunteer programs, and they get involved with National Youth Service Day and Nickelodeon's The Big Help. Many 4-H clubs are organized through schools. *(www.fourhcouncil.edu)*

Be Enthusiastic

One easy way to be a positive role model is to be enthusiastic about other people's accomplishments. Share in their successes. Let them know you are glad they won the award or got a good grade on the test. Cheer on your friend as she plays basketball. Then cheer on your friend who is in the chess club. (Just don't cheer too loudly while she's concentrating.) If your friend is hesitant to try out for the school play, encourage her.

Your conversation might go like this:

Lesley: "Hi, Anna!"

Anna: "Hi!"

Lesley: "Do you have a basketball game tonight?"

Anna: "Yeah, we do. Want to come watch?"

Lesley: "Well, I'm sort of thinking about auditioning for the school play, but I'm not sure I should . . ."

Anna: "Of course, you should. Go do it!"

Lesley: "Well, I'm not very good, and I don't know anyone else trying out. Maybe I'll come to your game instead."

Anna: "You can come to my game any time. Go try out. Remember how much fun we had doing that skit for Mr. Scheckner's class? You were great!"

Lesley: "I really like acting, but . . ."

Anna: "Go on and try out. I'll call you tonight to see how it went."

Anna helped Lesley by encouraging her to get involved in school. Lesley is working toward making the school a better place by getting involved in school activities.

You may have great intentions for improving your school, but some ideas are more suitable than others. Here's a list of "Ten Ideas Your Principal Will Probably *Not* Approve":

1. Build a hot tub in every classroom
2. Start school at 10:00 A.M. Dismiss at 1:30 P.M.
3. Let everyone bring their pets to school (horses included)
4. Have teachers serve hot fudge sundaes between classes
5. Have all the teachers give the answers along with the tests

6. Have each student picked up by a personal limousine instead of the school bus
7. Forbid teachers from assigning homework
8. Fly the students to Disneyland on a weekly basis
9. Give each student a $300 weekly clothing allowance
10. Provide extra food for cafeteria food fights

It's true. Your principal probably would never approve these ideas. She would be excited about other, more practical, ideas you have for making school a better place to be. Make a list of suggestions and present them to the principal. You might be surprised at how glad your principal is to have students looking to make positive improvements.

Action Plan

Draw posters to publicize school activities. Get some friends together and make motivational posters for your school. To make the posters extra special, glue on candy bars that tie in with your theme.

For example:

- *(Smarties* candy*)* "SMARTIES use the library often. Check out the new books on display today."
- *(Mints)* "You are worth a MINT to our school. Sign up to be a student council rep."

- *(Airheads)* "AIRHEADS miss out on great opportunities. Fill your head with knowledge."
- *(Good & Plenty)* "Buy hot lunch! GOOD & PLENTY food available at the lunch counter today."
- *(Crunch* bar*)* "Come to the volleyball game after school. We'll CRUNCH our opponents."
- *(Snickers)* "Don't SNICKER. Getting involved in school is cool."
- *(Whatchamacallit)* "It doesn't matter WHAT-CHAMACALLIT. The library or resource center is a great place to work on your book report."

Be Nice to Teachers

Have you ever looked at school from a teacher's viewpoint? You only have to turn in one English paper, while your teacher has to grade over twenty papers. You ask one question about fractions. Your teacher answers hundreds of math-related questions. You can make your school a better place to be by thinking about your teachers. If you are a good student, they have more energy to teach instead of having to handle discipline problems.

Try This!

Here are five quick tips on how to be a good student and make your teacher's job easier:

- Sit near the front of the class. It's easier to pay attention, and your teacher will appreciate seeing your smiling face!

- Occasionally do some extra-credit work. This improves your grade, plus you'll learn something extra.
- Have all the supplies you need for class. Plan ahead to have pencils sharpened and enough paper for assignments. You'll be able to get right to work instead of disrupting class as you borrow school supplies.
- When in doubt . . . look about! If you don't know what to do, look around. Are people getting out their math books? Is everyone reading quietly? Are there directions on the board?
- Pay attention and ask "good" questions. There is a saying, "There are no stupid questions," but there are. If your teacher is explaining the Civil War, it's not the time to ask when the pep assembly will start.
- Being a good student improves the atmosphere at your school. You might even be given some unusual opportunities. I was asked by a magazine to write an article about the "Do's and Don'ts of Teaching Children." It was supposed to give teachers ideas about how to be better teachers. Me? A kid giving advice to teachers? It happens! Here's what I wrote:

The Do's and Don'ts of Teaching Children

Last month I met the perfect teacher. From the minute I walked into her classroom, I knew I would like her. I'm in a program where once a week I go to a nearby high school for one hour of science. We have four weeks of chemistry and four weeks of biology. The chemistry session was disorganized. The teacher wasn't prepared.

Then I met Mrs. Chrissy for biology. Everything changed. She stood at the door and greeted us with a big smile. All of us were a little nervous being in a high school with lots of older kids. Her smile helped me feel safe as well as glad to be there. She gave out some information, but then let us get right into the activity. I couldn't believe my friend Alison Leake and I were excited about using a cotton swab to check the germs inside a toilet in the restroom. But Mrs. Chrissy was so enthusiastic that we happily collected toilet germs! A few weeks later we got to dissect squid. Again, Mrs. Chrissy was so excited that everyone forgot about being grossed out and started cutting away.

I know teachers have lots to think about, but it helps if they are prepared. Believe me, I can tell right away if a teacher isn't ready for the lesson. Sometimes teachers tell us, "Read a book while I get ready." Mrs. Chrissy always had the supplies laid out. She supervised high school students who worked in groups with us elementary students. Each older student knew exactly what to do, so we didn't have to wait while they got organized.

Because Mrs. Chrissy had things for us to do, the kids who normally caused trouble didn't have a chance to goof off. That makes the class more fun for me. Sometimes I think teachers are too lenient. They let kids get away with being rude or not doing the work. I try to work hard at school, and sometimes it bothers me to see all the teacher's attention go to the kids causing trouble. Here's what my friend Alison thinks about discipline: "What I have noticed is that most teachers have different ways of disciplining their class. None of the six teachers I've had in my school years have had the same method. Lots of the punishment for acting up is unpleasant. First of all, you get extremely embarrassed when you have to go up front of everyone in class and flip a card or see your name written on the board. But my teacher now has a good way to teach kids to stop acting up without it being too upsetting. Whenever you disrupt the class, she'll give you three chances to straighten up. If you don't and you keep disturbing the class, she will fine you. FINE YOU? Yes, in class we earn money. We have jobs that we do, just like we would when we get older. If you get fined, it means you have to take 5, 10, 20, 30, or 40 dollars from your money. At the end of the school year she gives you candy depending on how much money you have in the bank. I think this is a really neat way to discipline kids."

Here are some other characteristics of a good teacher:

They have extra work for people who finish early, maybe worksheets or a fun activity. I like it when I can keep doing something if I have finished my regular assignment.

Funny teachers are great. I had two team teachers, Mrs. Hawes and Mrs. Nelson, who would pretend to be ballerinas dancing to music. If they had something important to tell us, they'd act it out like it was a commercial. Here's what Alison thinks about fun teachers: "When I rank a teacher, I look at if she is fun. Does everyone like doing the project? If the thing you are making seems new and exciting even if you did it a couple of weeks ago, that means the teacher must have changed the way to do it."

One thing I don't like about teachers is if they are irritated with one student, then they snap at the next student they talk to. I watch and if a teacher seems upset, I don't ask them a question until some time passes.

If there were three things to describe the perfect teacher, they would be:
funny
caring
reinforces good behavior

What advice would you give teachers? Maybe you could write a note to your teacher telling him or her what it is you like about their class. I bet you like it when teachers tell you positive things about yourself.

Say Thanks

When was the last time you thanked your teacher for letting you do a creative book report instead of writing a three-page essay? You probably haven't. We all forget that teachers work hard to make class interesting. Do you like getting compliments? So do your teachers! The next time you have a fun assignment or the teacher gives you free time to clean your locker, say thank you. It may be the boost he or she needs.

You probably have heard of Ruby Bridges. She was the first black child integrated into a white school. In 1960 schools were still segregated. Black children were only allowed to go to school with other black children. When Ruby was six years old, she came to William Frantz Elementary School. Teachers and parents were appalled at the thought of a black child attending their school. Armed guards had to walk with Ruby to school because people were so upset.

Only one teacher, Barbara Henry, agreed to teach Ruby. Ms. Henry was a new teacher at the school. She had teaching experience, but nothing could prepare her for what was to come. None of the other teachers wanted Ruby. Ms. Henry welcomed her with open arms.

Ms. Henry tried hard to teach her class of one student like any other. Parents removed all the other students, so Ms. Henry worked individually with Ruby. She advanced Ruby far beyond her grade level despite the crowd's jeers coming from outside the window.

Ms. Henry is my heroine because she stood up for Ruby. In one incident, the principal wanted to lower Ruby's test scores. Ms. Henry stood up to the principal and made things right. Ms. Henry was very courageous when she took Ruby into her class. She had to accept the mean words and cries from the crowd too.

Your teachers probably don't have to put up with people yelling outside their windows. But they do have to put up with students who come to class with a bad attitude. Help make your school a better place by being the kind of student who teachers enjoy teaching. And don't forget to say thanks!

Try This!

Here are some ways to be a better student:

- Say hi to people as you pass them in the hall.
- Help keep your school clean by making sure trash gets in the garbage can.

- Offer to help if a group needs people to paint signs or distribute flyers.
- Follow the rules. There's a reason why you shouldn't bring knives to school or wear tube tops.
- Get involved with student government. If you don't want to run for an office, support the kids who do hold leadership positions.
- Submit articles or pictures to your school newspaper.
- If your school doesn't have many extracurricular activities, start some on your own. Ask a favorite teacher how to get a special-interest club going.
- If you see someone sitting by themselves, make an effort to invite them to your group.
- Leave a funny note in your friend's locker.
- Encourage your friends to be role models.
- Plan service projects that get kids involved in helping others.
- Promote school spirit by encouraging kids to buy and wear school sweatshirts.
- Talk to the principal to make sure every sport and club is recognized. Sometimes groups such as the science club or foreign language club take a backseat to sports teams.
- If you know some kids are having trouble with a school project, organize a study group.

- As you go through the day, think about the people in Lifeboat #14. Ask yourself, "Is there some way I can help someone today?"
- Stick up for kids who get bullied. Report bullies to a trusted teacher.
- If your school has a parents' night, set up a childcare program so parents can bring younger children.

Sondra's Ways of Making a Difference

1. When I was in Africa, one principal asked if I wanted to see the school library. Of course, I said yes. Instead of a room filled with books, he showed me a small bookcase with three shelves of old, tattered books. That was the school library. He was proud that his students could read *The Cat in the Hat* and *Noah's Ark*. As soon as I got home, I talked to my Girl Scout troop and some friends. It wasn't long until I collected over three hundred books to send to Africa. I wrote a letter to the president of DHL Shipping, explaining that I had the books but no money to ship them. DHL shipped all the books for free! Thanks, DHL!

2. I saw a small ad in the paper, asking students to write about their favorite teacher. I entered a story about my fifth-grade teacher, Ms. Offutt. I won the contest and she got a $50 certificate

to buy books. It also made her feel good to know someone in her class appreciated her.

This Could Be You . . .

1. Fourth, fifth, and sixth graders at Pelican Island Elementary School have an unusual volunteer project. They're trying to help save the Florida scrub jay, an endangered bird. They even raised $64,000 to buy three lots so the birds have a natural place to live.
2. My friend Phenicia got involved for two weeks in a Lunch Pals program at our school. This program matches volunteers with students at our school who are in special classes. Sometimes the students need extra help learning, or they have a physical disability. Phenicia spent lunchtime with an eighth-grade girl who needed a little extra help. It's a sacrifice to be in the Lunch Pals program because you don't eat lunch with your regular friends. Here's what Phenicia said about the experience: "At the end of my two weeks in the Lunch Pals program, it wasn't just another thing to do. I learned to respect people with disabilities. I did before, but not this deeply. The Lunch Pals program made me realize how many opportunities there are to brighten someone's day, even if it is only for thirty minutes a day."

Action Plan

Celebrate Random Acts of Kindness Week at home, at school, or in your community. It usually falls on the second week of February. You can get details on *www.actsofkindness.org*. Our school gets everyone involved by making daily announcements over the intercom about positive character traits. Our school student-body president talks about what it means to be respectful and have empathy or integrity. Later in the day, eighth graders come to the classrooms and pass out narrow slips of paper that ask: What random acts of kindness have you done or seen today? Everyone fills out the forms, which are then collected. Volunteers connect all the slips of paper and make a long chain. The paper chain stretches all around the perimeter of the cafeteria ceiling, reminding us of all the wonderful things kids do. Could you do the same thing at your school?

Improve Your School

Before I left for Africa, I asked my friends at school to donate clean, used T-shirts. My classmates couldn't fly to Africa with me, but they could feel involved by donating shirts. I collected 140 T-shirts and took them along in a huge suitcase. At a remote children's home on Bugala Island, Uganda, we displayed them in the community room like in a store. This was a learning experience, because most of the kids had never been in a store before. The kids paid with pretend money (pieces of leaves) and got to pick out a shirt. One of the teachers told me it was the first time the kids had ever had a chance to make a choice about what they wore. In the past, the children had to take whatever hand-me-downs someone gave them.

I also brought along craft supplies such as paint, beads, and craft foam. I was shocked at one school to see that the children didn't even know how to take the caps off markers to draw pictures! They had never seen glue or made paper-bag puppets. My mom had

Did You Know?

Seventy-seven percent of all public middle schools had students participating in community service activities organized by the school.
The total number of middle school students participating in service learning projects is 5 million.

U.S. Department of Education, 1999

made a sample puppet and was making it "talk." They looked at her in amazement because they didn't understand the idea of a puppet. At another school I set out hundreds of beads. The girls loved making necklaces but didn't know how to use scissors to cut the string for the beads.

When I got back from my trip, I showed slides of my experiences. This helped my class see how their T-shirts made a difference in the lives of the African students.

Try This!

How about organizing a book drive at your school? You could send the books to an inner-city school or maybe a school in rural Appalachia. Your friends probably have lots of books they don't read anymore that they would be glad to donate. Just spread the word or make some flyers. You'll be amazed how people are willing to help a worthy cause. You just have to ask. Here are some other projects you could do at school:

1. Organize a book exchange. Students bring in books they have already read. Give out one coupon for every donated book. On a specific day, display all the books. Kids come in and exchange their coupons for new books. This helps you get "new" books without spending any money.

2. Instead of a book exchange, you could organize a video game exchange using the same format.

3. Some schools have family book sales. Families set up tables in a large room like the gym or cafeteria. Each participating family sets up a display of all their books. Other people come along and buy the books for fifty cents or one dollar.

4. Do you have crafty friends? Ask kids to make homemade craft items. Again, set up tables and let kids sell their items, giving a portion of the proceeds to the school for "extras."

5. Find out about all the after-school activities offered at your school. Participate in at least one activity. You'll soon find ways to be a role model while playing the clarinet or going out for the volleyball team.

6. During winter, see about "Decorating a Glove Tree." Set up a tree in a noticeable place at

Did You Know?

More than one in three of all teens start volunteering before the age of fourteen.

Teens are four times more likely to volunteer if someone asks them.

Independent Sector Study, 1996

school. Ask kids to bring in warm hats and gloves to "decorate" the tree. Then donate the warm things to a shelter.

7. Does your school have sweatshirts or T-shirts with your school name? If so, wear your shirt! If not, talk to the principal about having a contest to design a picture to put on the front of school T-shirts.

8. Tell your friends the story of Lifeboat #14. Ask them for ideas on how you can all work together and reach out to students who need help.

Wrapping It All Up

Here's how you can be a member of Lifeboat #14 at school:

S Support school programs. Is the wrestling team looking for people to make posters for an upcoming match? Stay after school and use your artistic talents. Bake cookies for the school fundraiser and show your school spirit.

C Care about others. Is a new kid sitting alone? Invite him to sit with you. Thank your teachers for making class interesting,

H Help kids who are struggling. Does a friend have trouble learning fractions? Invite her over for a study session. If you are home-schooled, help your little brother with his reading. Or offer to teach a class to the younger kids. Your parents would love to have you as a role model for your brothers and sisters.

O Organize volunteer activities in your school. Start a new club or support a club with few members. Start a recycling program. Collect hats for needy kids in the winter. Homeschool kids can do these things too. If your home-school group has parent meetings, organize some crafts or games so younger kids have something to do while parents talk.

O Others will follow. Be a positive role model. Set a good example and soon others will learn it's a great thing to help people.

L Look for a way to make a difference. Instead of complaining about the drab entrance to your school, see if you can get plants and shrubs donated. If you see a need . . . see what you can do to fill it.

Part 3

Making a Difference in Your Community . . . and the World

I never thought a simple phone call could result in a trip to Africa, television appearances, and national awards. I just wanted to let people know how great my dad is. To give you an idea of how my simple act of reaching out led to some incredible opportunities, here's a brief timeline.

Father's Day, 2000: A radio announcer says, "We have a $50 prize for anyone who calls up and tells us why their dad is great." I call in and tell about how my dad dresses up in silly costumes as he dances to Broadway show tunes. He plays "trained dolphin" in the swimming pool by doing tricks that I tell him to do. I win $50 but tell the announcer to donate the money to charity.

The day after Father's Day: The radio announcer asks my mom to meet with him. He's connected with a Christian relief organization called Childcare International. They want to know if I'd be their spokeschild and help promote their organization. I say yes!

Christmas Day, 2000: Our family flies to Kenya and Uganda, where I meet kids living in the group homes set up by Childcare International. We also see kids living alone because their parents had died.

January 2001: I start speaking at churches to get sponsors for the kids I met in Africa. Soon I'm speaking to service clubs, schools, and women's groups. My dad puts together a PowerPoint presentation for me so I can show pictures of the children I met.

April 2001: Fox TV awards me the Fox Kids Hero Award. I get a gold medal, and they film a commercial about my trip to Africa. The commercial is designed to encourage kids to reach out and help others.

November 2001: Baker Book House asks me to write two books, *You've Got What It Takes!* and this book.

November 22, 2001: On my birthday, General Motors gives me a brand-new Chevy truck to use for a year as my family travels around the country promoting Childcare International.

January 23, 2002: Because of my work with Childcare International, I am selected to carry the Olympic torch.

February 2002: I win the Prudential Spirit of Community Award and $1,000. The award means I get to fly back to Washington, D.C., for four days of activities.

February 2002: The Points of Light Foundation selects me as a Daily Points of Light winner.

February 2002: I get a letter saying I earned $2,500 for the Tiger Woods' Start Something program.

March 2002: S&S Worldwide, a large arts and crafts company, asks me to be their spokeschild. I get to travel around the country doing workshops for them and encouraging families to play together.

None of these opportunities would've happened if I hadn't made an effort to call the radio station and talk about my dad. By reaching out and making someone else feel good, I got to enjoy some incredible experiences. You might come across some situations where you see a need to fill. Step out and see what you can do. You'll never know what can happen!

As you volunteer, all sorts of new experiences open up. One time I was giving a speech at a church about the orphans I met in Africa. Afterward I talked to people, got some kids sponsored, and went home. It seemed like an ordinary presentation. A few days later, a lady from the Aid Association for Lutherans called and said, "Someone in our office heard you speak at church. We'd like to buy sixty backpacks for the children you spoke about. We have $1,200, so we'll fill each backpack with toothbrushes, markers, paper, puzzles, and other school supplies. Would that be okay?" What do you think I said? Of course it was okay! It also taught me that people want to help others. If you find a volunteer opportunity, more than likely you can also find other people who want to help you.

Action Plan

Would you like to win a trip to Washington, D.C., for you and your parents? It's possible if you fill out an entry form for the Prudential Spirit of Community awards. *(www.prudential.com/community)* Each year they select one middle schooler and one high schooler from each state. Since about 28,000 kids apply each year, I was thrilled to be selected as a middle school honoree in 2002. My family got to spend four days in Washington, D.C., and even had dinner at the Museum of Natural History. One of the speakers was Martin Sheen, whom we got to meet! I was amazed at the variety of volunteer projects the kids did. Some of them were:

- Raising $150,000 to buy bullet-proof vests for police dogs
- Collecting blankets for homeless people
- Reading books on tape for blind people
- Collecting more than 20,000 meals at Thanksgiving for the needy

Why Volunteer?

We've looked at ways to volunteer at home and school. Now let's see about "official" volunteering in your community. Why should you volunteer? You're probably already busy with lots of activities. It's easier to *not* get involved. Remember the people in Lifeboat #14? Think how easy it would have been to paddle away from the other drowning people. The people in Lifeboat #14 looked beyond themselves. They knew the importance of helping others.

Look at these ten reasons why it's important to volunteer:

1. It improves your community.
2. Volunteering gives you a feeling of accomplishment. You've done something positive.
3. You get to be with friends or make new friends.
4. Volunteering helps you learn about other people and how they live.

5. You might get school credit for the volunteer work you do.
6. You'll probably learn new skills that will help you the rest of your life.
7. You'll be a role model for other people.
8. Volunteering teaches you leadership skills.
9. You'll learn more about activities and events in your community.
10. It gives you something to do besides watching television!

As you look at ways to volunteer, it's easy to get overwhelmed with all the possibilities. Have you ever watched the show *Lizzie McGuire*? It revolves around a girl in middle school and all the crazy things that happen to her. In one episode, Lizzie is assigned a school project to do volunteer work in order to "make the world a better place." Lizzie takes this project seriously. She decides to save all the animals of the world, so she becomes a vegetarian. Naturally she is disgusted that her family and friends still eat hamburgers. Next Lizzie decides to save the forests of the world. She actually yells at a teacher for giving a pop quiz because that uses paper, which means trees were cut down. Lizzie protests people wearing leather and has very strict standards about how her parents recycle. Toward the end of the show, Lizzie realizes she can't do everything. It's too hard to save the whales, recycle toilet paper, adopt stray dogs, help the homeless, and save the ozone by not using hair spray. Take a lesson from Lizzie . . . find one area you are interested in and volunteer for that cause. Maybe you want to improve the conditions at your local animal shelter. Maybe you want to raise money to get new uniforms for your gymnastics team. Whatever it is, try to focus on one activity. Otherwise you'll be going crazy like Lizzie did.

Ten Volunteer Opportunities You Don't Want to Get Involved In!

1. *Tooth brusher at a crocodile ranch*
2. *Underarm hair counter*
3. *Judge for the smelliest sneaker contest*
4. *Bad breath evaluator*
5. *Elephant poop inspector*
6. *Dirty dishwater disposer*
7. *St. Bernard slobber collector*
8. *Pig cleaner after a greased-pig contest*
9. *Listener of one hundred parents giving their most boring lectures on good behavior*
10. *Confetti collector after the New Year's Eve party in Times Square*

As you get involved in volunteer activities, you'll find yourself learning new skills. A group of students in Kendall, Washington, live in a rural community. They have about thirty members that meet twice a month to work on service projects together. The group keeps busy baby-sitting for community members, cleaning up local parks, and helping people pack and move. They even learned how to say "Merry Christmas" in Russian, since several community members are Russian. Who would have thought learning Russian was a part of volunteering?

Here are ways to narrow down your volunteer opportunities. Which of these activities interest you? Check the top three.

___ Working with animals
___ Helping younger children
___ Helping senior citizens
___ Being outdoors
___ Working with computers
___ Improving the environment
___ Sports
___ Theatrical activities
___ Helping people with special needs

Great! You're narrowing your focus. Now that you have some idea about what you want to do, how will you find available opportunities? What do you do if you're interested in animals but there is no zoo in your area?

Try some of these ideas for finding places to volunteer:

Check the yellow pages in your phone book. Many communities have volunteer centers that match interested people with volunteer needs.

Ask a teacher or principal for ideas.

Call groups like the Girl Scouts, Boys and Girls Clubs, or the local hospital and see if they need volunteers.

Ask your friends what they do to volunteer.

Your church youth group leader might have some ideas.

Read the local newspaper. Many times there is a section called "Volunteer Opportunities." I just opened our paper and here are some volunteer opportunities listed:

- Play games, assist with arts and crafts, and read to residents of an assisted-living center
- Assist selling concessions at a local non-profit theater
- Help with clerical duties at a nonprofit center.

Call the local Humane Society if you want to work with animals.

See if your Chamber of Commerce office keeps a list of volunteer opportunities.

Simply ask an organization you are interested in if they use volunteers.

You'll also need to answer these questions:

How much time do you have to volunteer? Some activities require you to put in a minimum number of hours each week.

Do you need transportation? Is a bus available or will an adult have to drive you?

Are you the right age? Some places require you to be at least a certain age.

Will you volunteer alone or with a friend?

Will it cost you money? If so, how much?

What kind of supervision will you have? (That's what parents want to know.)

Is it "practical"? You can't take off and join the Peace Corps if you are twelve years old.

You're moving right along! Now that you have an idea where you want to volunteer, here are a few things to remember.

Ten Tips to Being a Great Volunteer

1. *Be on time. People are expecting you, so make sure you are there when you are expected.*
2. *Attend the orientation, if there is one. It will help you be a more informed volunteer.*
3. *Put your heart into what you are doing.*
4. *Realize not every part of volunteering is fun. You may need to wash dishes or stick stamps on 200 envelopes.*
5. *Be flexible. You'll learn more that way.*

6. *Do a little extra.* Try to add your special touch to your volunteer job.

7. *Think about other people's needs.* You're there to help, even if it is hard work.

8. *Recruit others.* If you enjoy volunteering, encourage your friends to get involved also.

9. *Take your "work" seriously.* Sure, you'll have fun, but know that what you are doing is important to other people.

10. *Give volunteering some time.* You might get involved in a project that isn't as exciting as you thought it would be. Hang in there. You may find you like what you are doing after you get more comfortable in the situation. Galatians 6:9 says, "Let us not get tired of doing what is right, for after a while we will reap a harvest of blessing if we don't get discouraged and give up."

As you look at ways to volunteer, remember that it doesn't mean raising $30,000 for a new library. You can help improve your community by picking up some litter as you walk to school or cleaning up your dog's poop from the sidewalk! Our neighbor, Sally Warrington, loves walking through the park behind our house. On one path, a small wooden bridge crosses a ditch. The rain in Washington often makes the bridge slippery. Sally made a sign that said, "Caution! This bridge is VERY slippery." She put the note in plastic and thumbtacked it to the bridge. Anyone crossing the bridge read the sign and avoided slipping. See? She had the power to improve her community with a single piece of paper.

There are many times the Bible talks about helping other people. One of the best-known examples is the Good Samaritan. You probably remember the story. A man was walking to Jericho when he got beat up and robbed. As he lay on the road, a priest walked by, ignoring the hurt man. Then a Levite also passed him by. The poor man kept lying by the road until a Samaritan came by and took care of him. Jesus asked, "Which of these men was a neighbor to the hurt man?" Obviously it was the Samaritan, who took time to help someone in need. When we help people at home, at school, or in our community, it's the same as helping God. You can't send God a Christmas card or give him food, but you can help other people in his name.

Here's a "disclaimer" about volunteering. It's nice to help someone or some cause, especially when you get a warm and fuzzy feeling from it. But sometimes your volunteer experiences may not turn out the way you wanted them to. Our small-group Bible study heard about a homeless woman with five children. She finally got one tiny room in a motel. Our small group tried to find her a home. No one wanted to rent to her because she didn't have any money. Finally someone agreed to let her live in a big, four-bedroom house. It was like a dream come true. We all helped to paint it, wash windows, and collect furniture. We gave her our sofa and love seat so the family would have something to sit on. My mom gave the two teenagers money, and we went to garage sales so they could buy things for their room. Other people donated food and clothes. Our small group felt so good that this family had a nice house and could live a "normal" life. About nine months later, the landlord came to us and said he had to evict her because the house was such a mess. It's true. After she left, our small group went over to clean up. There were bugs all over the kitchen and bags of trash over six months old. The floors were covered in dirt. She hadn't paid her water bill, so the toilets and sink didn't work. You can imagine how that smelled. We actually hauled four big dump-truck loads of trash to the dump. I felt sad thinking about how we all tried to help her have a nice clean house and she didn't care. Our small group talked about how we did what God wanted us to do. It's just that this lady wasn't capable of taking care of what we gave her. There may be a time when you volunteer and the result isn't what you expected. Just do what you know is right. Most of the time your volunteer efforts will be totally positive!

Ten "Too Good to Be True" Volunteer Opportunities

1. *You volunteer to let a reporter follow you around as you enjoy an all-expense-paid shopping spree at the mall.*

2. You set it up so all your friends get to be dropped off at school each morning in a limousine.
3. Your teacher didn't print enough math tests. You volunteer to get an automatic A instead of taking the test.
4. You are selected as a new-ride tester for Disneyland.
5. A cleaning company chooses you as a volunteer to have their maids clean your room every day.
6. The producer of Lizzie McGuire calls and asks if you want to volunteer to have a part on the show.
7. A company asks you to test their sunscreen and sends you and your friends to Hawaii.
8. The president wants you to volunteer by spending a day with him, offering suggestions on how to run the country.
9. You're asked to design a new amusement park.
10. A candy company wants you to be their official volunteer taste tester.

Try This!

Let's look at some volunteer opportunities that tie in with your specific interests.

If you are interested in animals:

Keep birdfeeders stocked in your backyard.

See if a local Humane Society will let you walk or play with dogs for exercise.

With your parents' permission, look into raising a puppy as a Seeing Eye dog for the blind. Puppies need to be raised around families to help them be better Seeing Eye dogs.

If you are confident around horses, many stables need volunteers to help with therapeutic riding lessons for handicapped kids.

Is there a nature habitat or wildlife center in your area? They might need volunteers.

Many nursing homes look for volunteers to bring in cute bunnies or calm pets.

Check if your community has a pet-food bank for low-income people. Donate pet food so people with limited money can feed their pets.

If you are the dramatic type (love to put on plays and sing and dance):

Help put on birthday parties for younger kids.

Get involved in local theater productions. See about auditioning for a local college's summer-stock program.

Organize a neighborhood talent show. Charge admission and give the money to charity.

Get your friends to put on skits or a musical concert. Perform for nursing homes or day care centers.

Are you physically active? If you like moving and being on the go, these activities are for you!

See if you can help coach a young kids' sports team.

If you play on a sports team, ask the coach about offering a teaching clinic for younger players.

Ask the local Parks department if they need help planting trees or clearing trails.

Organize fun games for neighborhood kids.

Take a neighbor's dog for walks.

Does your school have flowers? See if you can volunteer to keep them watered over summer vacation.

Do you like helping people? Perhaps you want to work directly with other people. Here are some ways to volunteer:

See if you can help read books to kids at your library's summer-reading program.

Offer to sit outside at a nursing home on a sunny day and talk with or read to residents.

Call day camps to see if they use junior counselors.

Organize a neighborhood carnival where kids can work together building carnival booths.

Perhaps your family can get involved with the Meals on Wheels program. You'll deliver meals

Did You Know?

Want to help the environment? Stop using wooden chopsticks! Well, if you live in China, you should. Experts say that each year, twenty-five million trees are cut down to produce forty-five billion pairs of wooden chopsticks in China. Many trees could be saved if people used personal chopsticks instead of the throwaway kind.

to shut-ins and spend some time talking with them.

How about this idea? Joining the Girl Scouts is a great way to get started in volunteering. The Girls Scouts have always had a reputation for volunteering. Some projects include working in shelters for the homeless, doing community health drives, and helping immigrants get settled. When not volunteering, Girl Scouts go river rafting, biking, hiking, and do other fun activities. If you don't have a troop in your area, you can become a Juliette Scout and work on badges on your own. That's what I'm doing! Since we're traveling the country for a year, I have my own "troop" as a Juliette Scout. To get more information, look up *www.girlscouts.org*.

Thinking of getting more involved in your church? Churches have many areas where volunteers can make a big difference. Do any of these ideas appeal to you?

If you're artistic, ask to decorate or organize church bulletin boards.

The nursery at your church probably needs people to wash all the baby toys each week. This may not be glamorous, but it is a job needing to be done. Babies put everything in their mouths. Nursery workers clean the toys often to help kill germs.

Does your church have a Vacation Bible School in the summer? Ask if you can help with younger kids.

Ask the church secretary if she needs help stuffing envelopes or folding bulletins.

Organize a church spruce-up day where volunteers plant flowers, wash windows, and get the church looking spotless.

Your youth group leader might need help setting up a room for meetings.

Check if your church offers missions trips or volunteer programs in the community. Sometimes these programs are already set up, so all you need to do is sign up and go. (Well, you better check with your parents before you register to go on a missions trip to Africa!)

Organize a few fundraising activities and sponsor a child from a Third World country. Naturally, I think you should sponsor a child through Childcare International, but there are other worthwhile organizations also. Sponsoring a child means that child has food, medical attention, and a chance to go to school. Here's an excerpt from Childcare's newsletter that describes how life changing it is to sponsor a child.

Kato and his sister, Babirye, lived alone. When their father and mother died within months of one another, the double tragedy left them numb. Their world seemed to come to a standstill. What were they to do? They had nowhere to go and no one to care for them. Fear became their constant companion. They had no food or chance to get help. But thanks to the faithful support of Childcare International's friends, these children found a new life. When Michael Masembe, Childcare's Uganda director, heard about them, he sought them out, and promised: "We will find you sponsors in the United States. You will be the first children for our very new children's homes." That promise turned the fear that filled the hearts of Kato and Babirye to hope. Today they're living in the Eleanor Jones Home, the first one to be completed. Life for them has taken on new meaning, as they enjoy their new friends, and the care and security of a home. Instead of living alone—hungry and afraid—they enjoy the care they receive. They go to school, do chores, and have a chance to play—something every child should experience.

For more information about Childcare International, call 800-553-2328 or see *www.childcare-intl.org.*

This Could Be You . . .

1. Ruby Franklin is only ten years old but is a very good piano player. She visits nursing homes and plays ragtime and jazz for the residents. Ruby even won a Fox Kids Hero Award for her efforts!

2. Last Christmas there was an article in the paper about a seventeen-year-old boy named Misionare. He worked at a part-time job and saved six paychecks to buy $600 worth of Christmas presents for his family. After an afternoon of shopping, Misionare headed to a local Boys and Girls Club to serve dinner to needy families. Suddenly he saw a thief running away with a purse stolen from a woman. Misionare set down his Christmas presents and raced after the thief. He stopped the thief and threw him on the ground until others came to help. Misionare went back to get his presents . . . they were gone! Someone had stolen them. He was so sad, he sat on the curb and cried. Misionare was like the people in Lifeboat #14. He took a risk and helped someone else. But the story does have a happy ending. Police officers took up a collection and gave Misionare $800.

3. My friends Krista, Jane, and Mandy wanted to help the people in New York after September 11. They got themselves organized and started making friendship bracelets out of red, white, and blue embroidery floss. Then they contacted a local grocery store to see if they could sell the

bracelets in front of the store. It wasn't long until they raised $1,100!

4. St. John's Lutheran Church in Decatur, Illinois, started a small volunteer-run living Nativity many years ago that now uses more than 250 volunteers! The first weekend in December, volunteers dress in costumes and set up a living Nativity. Several "scenes" are set up, ranging from Mary and the angel to the inn and manger. They even have sheep and horses walking around! Visitors slowly drive their cars by the scenes and listen to an audiotape recording explaining the story of Christ's birth.

Sondra's Ways of Making a Difference

1. Our family heard that a church needed volunteers to help serve Easter dinner to homeless families. I pictured myself easily scooping up mashed potatoes as hungry people said thank you to me. Instead, the volunteer organizer asked us to come back after the meal was served. I ended up mopping mashed potatoes off the floor and cleaning the bathrooms. I saw that those jobs really needed to be done. The best part of the day was when a homeless woman came late. She had three little girls with her. We served her food, and I gave her daughters each a stuffed Easter bunny I'd brought along. Seeing their smiles made up for cleaning toilets!

2. I recently got to attend a gigantic trade show in Anaheim. Over two thousand booths were set up, displaying all the latest craft items. This trade show was definitely a hit with me because I loved seeing all the new beads, craft kits, and candles. At one booth, the salesperson asked if I wanted to make a decorated magnet. He handed me a plain, thin piece of magnetic material about the size of a mouse pad. Then he handed me several sheets of rub-off transfers. The craft involved rubbing the transfer onto the magnetic piece. After using two or three pictures off the sheet, the salesperson tossed the rest of the transfers away. It shocked me because there were so many pictures left. I knew the kids in Africa would love using these transfers. I asked the salesperson to save me all the other used sheets. The next day when I came back, he handed me a huge stack of transfer sheets to send to Africa. He wanted to give his customers new sheets, yet I knew the used sheets were perfect for kids looking to make a fun project. All I had to do was ask him to help. Besides, "One man's trash is another man's treasure!"

Action Plan

Help Childcare International, the Christian agency that asked me to be their spokeschild. This organization has a great program that involves animals and helps kids in Africa. The Kids to Kids program lets you pay $25 to buy a "kid" (a baby goat) for a child in Africa. The children learn to take care of their goats, which also give them fresh milk to drink. To sign up, just go to the Childcare web site at *www .childcare-intl.org* or have an adult call 800-553-2328.

Moneymaking Activities

Many times you'll hear about a group or an organization that needs help. Maybe they need new computers or food to feed homeless people. You'd like to help out, but your allowance only goes so far. At first I was hesitant to ask people for money, but now . . . hey! I know the money goes to a good cause, so I just boldly ask for what I want.

Naturally there will be times when you get turned down, but just keep on trying. What if you ask a store for free party decorations so you can have a party for homeless kids . . . and they say no?

I'm sure you'd feel bad, but be realistic. Did the ceiling just fall down on you? Did your head suddenly pop off because a store manager said no? Will your dog ignore you when you get home? No. You simply had one person tell you they couldn't help out. When my agent sent out a proposal for my third book, *You've Got What It Takes!* ten publishers rejected it. But the eleventh publisher (Baker Book

House!) offered me a two-book contract. That's why you're reading this book now. It would have been easy to give up and say, "No one wants to publish my book."

I've found that people really want to help good causes. Make sure you have a clear idea about what you need when you go to other people and ask them for donations. Maybe even tell the story of Lifeboat #14. Explain that you want to be a member of Lifeboat #14 and help make the world a better place.

Try This!

In some situations, instead of asking businesses or adults for money, you can come up with creative ways to raise money on your own. Here are some ideas to help you earn money to give to a worthy cause. (Of course you need to check with your parents before doing any of these activities.)

- Find jobs as a mother's helper. You play games and read to young children while their mother is still in the house.
- Gather a few friends together and offer to wash a neighbor's car in their driveway. You bring buckets, rags, and soap. They provide a dirty car and the water from their hose.
- Let neighbors know you are available to walk their dogs or take care of their pets if they are out

of town. You might get paid to feed a neighbor's fish!

- Earn money watering a neighbor's plants or lawn when they are on vacation.

- Here's a practical idea. If your neighborhood has curbs on the street, offer to spray paint the house address on the curb. Use a stencil to get a clear pattern. These numbers are helpful to police and fire trucks in finding houses in emergencies. Make sure to have an adult help watch for traffic.

- Go door to door, asking if people want to donate items to a garage sale. Often people are glad to get rid of furniture or clothes and gladly give things to you for a good cause.

- Do you play an instrument or have skills in a sport? Offer lessons or tutoring to younger children.

- Parents need help with preschool birthday parties. Earn money by being a party assistant. Help kids play games and avoid spilling juice.

- Many people neglect their streetside mailboxes. Offer to wash their mailboxes and touch up the numbers and names.

- Make up a series of "No Special Reason" cards. Sell them to friends and neighbors who enjoy sending out personalized cards.

- Offer to make garage sale signs for people. Often they get so busy pricing and organizing their "stuff," they don't have time to make signs.

Charge extra to put up or take down the garage sale signs.

- If you live in an area with lots of people, never underestimate the power of an old-fashioned lemonade stand on a hot day.
- Write up the story of Lifeboat #14 on a postcard or flyer. Explain what cause you are trying to help. Give the information to family and friends, asking them for a donation.

All the organized volunteer programs in the world can't make up for the impact you make by being friends with a lonely or needy person. Do you know someone who doesn't have many friends? Is there someone you know who needs a ride to your youth group meetings? Ask an adult if you can pick them up. Taking time to be with someone is often more valuable than giving them an expensive gift.

This Could Be You . . .

My older sister, Trina, was part of her youth group's outreach team. She visited an elderly Mexican lady once a week, just to talk and share. Trina would also get groceries and deliver them to the woman. One day the lady wanted to show her thanks by making Trina an authentic Mexican meal. Trina watched as the woman made the meal. The problem was the woman got confused and poured chocolate syrup over the enchilada instead of tomato sauce. Yes, Trina ate it!

Sondra's Way of Making a Difference

It's easy for me to quickly spend my money on books or fun things for my room. So I've come up with a way to manage my money so I can spend, save, and tithe. The next time you go to a 7-Eleven store, ask your parents for a large 3-Flavor Slurpee. (Tell them it's for a good cause!) After you drink the Slurpee, wash out the container so it isn't sticky. You'll see it has three distinct compartments. Label the sections "Savings," "Tithe," and "Spending." When I get money, I go to my cup and put 10 percent in the tithe section. I divide the rest of the money between savings and spending. That way I have money available to help out at church, as well as to save for more expensive items.

Action Plan

Is there something you'd like to buy that would help you improve the world? Would you like a new clarinet so you could play music at nursing homes? Do you need a new bike to help you get to your grandmother's house and help her with chores? Would you like to go to a sports camp that helps you learn to coach younger kids? Here's a way to earn up to $5,000! It takes some work, but it's worth it. The next time you go to a Target store, ask for a brochure on their Start Something program. You can also go online at *www.startsomething.target.com*. Start Something is a program run by Tiger Woods, who wants to help kids between the ages of eight and seventeen. You begin by registering online. You'll get a set of ten activities that take about two hours each to do. (You can set your own pace, though.) The activities are designed to help you decide on your interests and skills. As you complete each set of activities, you move to the next step. After all ten steps are done, you can apply for scholarships that give you up to $5,000! Tiger Woods gives away $300,000 each year! Some kids get all excited about the program but forget to actually DO the activities and turn them in. Believe me, it's worth it when you get a letter saying, "Congratulations! You've received $2,500 from Tiger Woods!" I did the steps and got $2,500 to buy a really nice laptop computer.

Ways to Change Your World

Here are some places you can find out about other volunteer opportunities. Many magazines and web sites describe how kids help their school and community with worthwhile service projects. Reading about other kids might inspire you to get busy with your own volunteer project!

Youth Service America—This web site is a starting point for any kids wanting to get involved with volunteering. You'll find links to lots of great sites that offer tips on how to serve your community. *www.servenet.org*

Time for Kids—Time magazine is known for its information and news from around the world. Now look up *Time for Kids, www.timeforkids .com.* Click on "Fix the World" and see different ways to make an impact at school or in your community.

Points of Light—Need some inspiration about making a difference? Look up *www.pointsoflight.org* and read stories of amazing children and adults. A different Points of Light winner is featured every day. If you or someone you know has made a difference by helping others, nominate them to be a Points of Light winner.

Prudential Spirit of Community Award—This national program honors youth who make a difference in the world. Nominate someone or read about past winners. You'll be impressed with the creativity people show as they try to improve the world. *www.prudentialspirit.com/community*

The Caring Institute—Just as the name implies, the Caring Institute honors people who care about the environment, other people, and even animals. They also offer awards to kids and adults who volunteer. *www.caring-institute.org*

Guideposts for Kids—Your parents probably read *Guideposts* magazine. There's a magazine for kids called *Guideposts for Kids*. Look on their web site, *www.gp4k.com* under "Cool Kids." You'll read about how kids make a difference by volunteering.

Discovery Girls magazine—This magazine, geared for preteen girls, spotlights kids who volunteer.

You'll also find helpful hints on earning money or starting a business. *www.discoverygirls.com*

American Girl magazine—Preteen girls will enjoy all the great ideas on making friends or doing crafts. Each issue also features girls doing volunteer work. Their web site is also fun to use. *www.americangirl.com*

Brio magazine—This Christian magazine for teen girls has practical and fun information about growing up. You'll read about girls going on missions trips, helping at churches, and volunteering in the community. After looking at their web site, you'll probably want to order their magazine. *www.briomag.com*

Girl Power—The web site *www.girlpower.gov* features great articles and games. Read inspirational stories about women who helped change the world. Lots of ideas on how to be a strong, confident girl.

Girl Scouts—If you're a Girl Scout, you probably have had plenty of opportunities to volunteer with your troop. Even if you are not a Girl Scout, their web site has great ideas on making a difference. *www.girlscouts.org*

Roots and Shoots—Do you like animals? Look up Jane Goodall's web site and learn about the Roots and Shoots program to help animals and the environment around the world. *www.jane goodall.org*

Kids Hall of Fame—You've heard of the Baseball Hall of Fame, but did you know there's a Kids Hall of Fame? They publish a magazine that describes how kids are making a difference and doing amazing things. *www.TheKidsHallofFame.com*

The Big Help—This is a campaign by Nickelodeon to encourage kids to volunteer in their community. Call 212-258-7080. *www.nick.com*

American Red Cross—Since the founding of Junior Red Cross in 1917, young people have been involved in volunteer activities. They can become international pen pals, organize blood drives, train in first aid, and serve as mentors to younger students. *www.redcross.org*

National Recreation and Park Association—This organization offers many opportunities for kids to volunteer. Contact your local Parks and Rec office or look at their web site. *www.nrpa.org*

Boys and Girls Club of America—Do you like to play basketball or make crafts? You could volunteer with a Boys and Girls Club in your area. *www.bgca.org*

Make a Difference Day—This national program inspires and rewards volunteers. This event is held on the last Saturday in October, and individuals and groups can get involved in thousands of different volunteer activities. *www.make adifferenceday.com*

You've Got What It Takes!—Need a little boost to help you get motivated to volunteer? My book *You've Got What It Takes!* helps you set goals and learn how to reach your dreams. If you need encouragement to try something new, this book will give you the tips and inspiration you need.

Wrapping It All Up

C Come together to work on projects. Get friends or neighbors involved. It's more fun to be with other people, and you'll get more done.

O Organize! You might have a great idea to raise money for a worthy cause, but you'll need to be organized. Make checklists, ask for help, and keep to a schedule. Research how other people in similar situations volunteered.

M Make volunteer opportunities happen. Look around and see what you can do to help. If your school doesn't have a volunteer or service club, see if you can put one together.

M Motivate others to get involved. If you enjoy helping sell tickets at the community theater, invite other friends to help. If people see you are doing something worthwhile, they'll want to help also.

U Unleash your talents and try new things. Volunteering is a great chance to learn about different careers. You get to meet new people and do things you haven't done before. Maybe you'll find yourself training dolphins or writing a newsletter for your youth group.

N New friends can be found through volunteering. You'll meet people with the same interests as you work on projects together. Maybe your best friend doesn't enjoy chess. You can still be friends with her, yet also meet new friends as you coach a younger kids chess club.

I Investigate different volunteer opportunities. Read the paper, ask teachers, or call different organizations. Ask what volunteer jobs you could do.

T Think about your commitment. Volunteer organizations will come to depend on you. Make sure you have the time to volunteer. Will you need transportation? Will you be so busy you neglect school work?

Y You can change your world! Get involved and help make the world a better place by volunteering in your community. Be a part of Lifeboat #14.

Conclusion

Congratulations! You've finished reading this book. Now it's your turn to begin your volunteer experiences. So keep an eye open for unique and exciting opportunities.

I've been involved in volunteering since I passed out crayons in preschool! My most exciting experience was visiting Africa. When I got back home, I wanted to do more to help the children I'd met. After praying about it, my parents and I decided to take a volunteer trip around the U.S. to promote Childcare International. Chevy even gave us a truck to use for the year! We bought a fifth wheel and were on our way.

Living in an RV is harder than I'd expected. My bed is about two feet wide, and my closet is tiny! I don't have much extra space for stuffed animals or books. We do have a microwave, refrigerator, freezer, and stove, though.

Every Sunday I speak at a different church about Childcare International. It's an eye-opening experience to see how people worship in different ways and places. Some churches meet in tiny rented school buildings. I even gave a presentation at a Yogi Bear campground in Warrens, Wisconsin, where people sat in golf carts during the church service!

I do miss my friends, but I know what we're doing is helping many children in developing countries. This is a once-in-a-lifetime opportunity to volunteer on a long-term project.

You may not be able to take a year and travel around the country, but you *can* change the world by volunteering at your home, school, or community.

Happy volunteering!

Answers for Candy Quiz

1. 3 Musketeers
2. Clark Bar
3. Big Hunk
4. Mounds
5. Whatchamacallit
6. Peppermint Patty
7. Almond Joy
8. Rocky Road
9. Baby Ruth
10. Mars
11. Payday
12. Junior Mints
13. Milk Duds
14. Skor

Thirteen-year-old Sondra Clark is the author of *Craft Fun with Sondra, Wearable Art with Sondra,* and *You've Got What It Takes!* She is also a recipient of the national Fox TV Kids Hero Award and the Prudential Spirit of Community Award, speaker for churches and conference groups, and the spokeschild for Childcare International.

Another book
from
SONDRA

Here's all the stuff you need to know to start making your dreams come true. Sondra helps you set goals and stick to them, be positive, deal with your friends, take responsible risks, be a more fun you, and give it your best shot.

Packed with fun sidebars, "silly quizzes," quotes from celebrities like Michelle Kwan and Mia Hamm, and more, *You've Got What It Takes!* will help you accomplish what you dream of doing and become all that you hope to be.